Poppy
the Piano
Fairy

Special thanks to
Narinder Dhami

ISBN: 978-0-545-10624-5

12 11 10 9 8 7   13 14/0

Printed in the U.S.A.

First Scholastic Printing, January 2010

Poppy
the Piano
Fairy

by Daisy Meadows

SCHOLASTIC INC.

New York   Toronto   London   Auckland

Sydney   Mexico City   New Delhi   Hong Kong

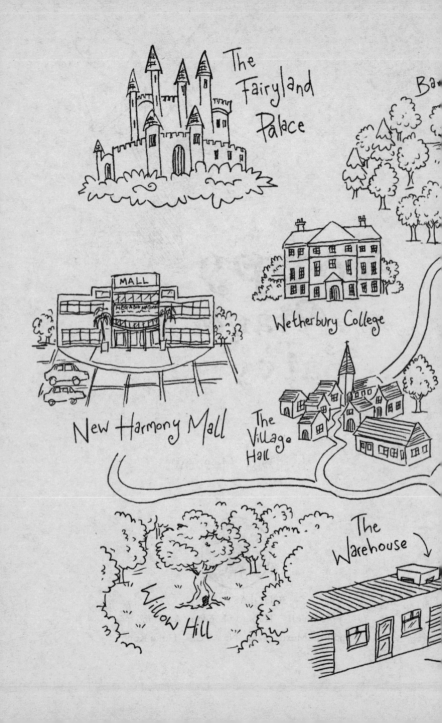

I'm through with frost, ice, and snow.
To the human world I must go!
I'll form my cool Gobolicious Band.
Magical instruments will lend a hand.

With these instruments, I'll go far.
Frosty Jack, a superstar.
I'll steal music's harmony and its fun.
Watch out, world, I'll be number one!

Contents

A Musical Message

"Ooh, I love to dance!" Rachel Walker sang along to the radio, pretending her hairbrush was a microphone. "When I hear the music, my toes start tapping and my fingers start snapping!"

Kirsty Tate, Rachel's best friend, grinned and grabbed her own hairbrush.

"I can't stop dancing!" She joined in on the chorus.

The girls tried to do a complicated dance routine as they sang, but Kirsty went left and Rachel went right and they ended up bumping into each other! Laughing, they collapsed onto Kirsty's bedroom carpet.

"It's really hard to sing and dance at the same time," said Rachel as the song ended. "I know," Kirsty agreed. "I don't think we'd be very good in a band, Rachel!"

"That was The Sparkle Girls with their new single, 'Can't Stop Dancing,'" the radio DJ announced as Kirsty and Rachel sat up. "And if anyone out there thinks they could make it big as a pop star, too, why not come out and audition for the National Talent Competition next weekend?"

Rachel and Kirsty glanced at each other.

"That sounds cool!" Rachel said.

"One lucky singer or band will win a recording contract with MegaBig Records," the DJ went on. "So remember — come out to the New Harmony Mall next weekend, and maybe one day I'll be playing *your* songs on my show!"

"The New Harmony Mall is only a few miles from Wetherbury," Kirsty said dreamily. "I'm sure Mom or Dad would take us to watch the competition if we asked them."

"That would be great," Rachel replied eagerly. "We're pretty lucky that the contest takes place before I go home." Rachel was staying with Kirsty during school break, and her parents would be coming to pick her up at the end of the following weekend.

"And now here's Leanne Roberts with her new song, 'Magical Moments,'" said the DJ.

"Oh, I love this one," Rachel said, turning the radio up a little.

"Me, too," Kirsty agreed. She smiled as Rachel began dancing around the room. "Maybe we should enter the Talent Competition ourselves!" Rachel laughed. "I'm a horrible singer!" she said, making a face. "But I bet we'd have a lot of fun singing along with our friends in Fairyland, wouldn't we?" Kirsty nodded. She and Rachel shared a very special and magical secret. They were good friends with the fairies! They had visited Fairyland many times. But the girls had never told anyone about their fairy adventures, not even their parents.

"Life is special, life is fun," Kirsty sang along to the radio as Rachel twirled around their beds. "Look for the magic in everyone!"

Then, unexpectedly, the music changed. Kirsty and Rachel stared at each other in surprise as the bouncy tune of "Magical Moments" suddenly became a much sweeter and softer melody.

"Kirsty and Rachel!" a tiny, silvery voice sang from the radio. "Can you hear me, girls?"

Rachel and Kirsty could hardly believe their ears.

"There's a fairy speaking to us through the radio!" Kirsty gasped.

"Yes, we can hear you!" Rachel declared, breathless with excitement.

"Girls, I'm so glad you were listening to music. That made it possible for me to contact you immediately!" the fairy said, sounding very relieved. "My name is Poppy the Piano Fairy, and I'm one of the seven Music Fairies."

"Hello, Poppy!" said Rachel.

"Is everything OK in Fairyland?" asked Kirsty.

"Oh, girls, we're in terrible trouble!"
the fairy went on anxiously. "We need
your help right away. Jack Frost and his
goblins are invading Fairyland's Royal
School of Music!"

Rachel and Kirsty were horrified. Jack
Frost was a very mischievous fairy. He
and his goblins were always
causing trouble in
Fairyland, and
the girls often
helped their
fairy friends
outsmart them and
prevent them from making mischief.

"What's Jack Frost up to now?" Rachel
wanted to know.

"Well, the school's a very special place
because it's where all the fairies come to

learn music," Poppy expla[...] vo[...]
where we Music Fairies ke[...] qu[...]
musical instruments. They [...]e imp[...]
because they make music [...] on[...]
harmonious in Fairyland [...] girl[...]
human world. We think J[...] glit[...]
to steal the magic instrum[...] and[...]
need help to stop him fro[...]
fingers on them! Can you [...]
Fairyland immediately?"

"Of course we can,"
Rachel declared.

"We'll be there in a
flash!" Kirsty added.

"Thank you so
much," Poppy replied
gratefully. "Please
hurry!"

Instantly, the fairy's

faded away. Rachel and Kirsty
ly opened the gold lockets the
ther Fairies had given them after
of their adventures together. Each
arefully took a pinch of the
ring fairy dust from inside the locket
hen sprinkled it over herself.

A whirl of
sparkling
rainbow colors
surrounded the
girls, and they
suddenly felt
themselves
tumbling
through the air.
With each turn
they shrank
smaller and

smaller until they were fairy-size. They even had wings!

"I just hope we're in time to stop Jack Frost!" Kirsty cried.

Music School
Mayhem

ROYAL SCHOOL
OF MUSIC

A few moments later, the bright rainbow
colors swirled away, and the girls found
themselves outside a tall white house next
to the Fairyland palace. There was a gold
sign on the gate with ROYAL SCHOOL OF
MUSIC written on it in pink letters.

The wooden doors of the school were

wide open. As Rachel and Kirsty hurried over, a fairy rushed out to meet them. She looked very stylish in her black pants and pink shirt, with a hat perched on top of her red corkscrew curls.

"Girls, you're here!" the fairy exclaimed, looking very relieved. "I'm Poppy the Piano Fairy."

"Where are Jack Frost and his goblins now?" Kirsty asked as Poppy ushered them inside the school.

"They're on their way to the practice room," Poppy explained quickly. "That's where we keep the magic musical

instruments. We have to hurry!" She
zoomed up the winding
spiral staircase.
"Follow me!"
Rachel and
Kirsty whizzed
after Poppy. At
the top of the
stairs, the fairy
stopped,
hovering in the
open doorway
of a large
room. As the
girls caught up
with Poppy, they
gasped at the chaotic
scene before them.

The practice room was a complete mess. Cupboard doors stood open, chairs and music stands had been overturned, and there were various musical instruments and pages of sheet music scattered all over the floor. In the middle of the mayhem were seven goblins. One of them held an ice wand.

They were standing around a tangled
heap of musical instruments, gazing
eagerly at them with wide, greedy eyes.
Unlike the others, these instruments
glowed with a faint, magical sparkle.
Kirsty and Rachel could see a beautiful
grand piano in the middle of the jumble.

"Those are our magic instruments!"
Poppy whispered in dismay.

As Poppy, Rachel, and Kirsty raced
into the room, the goblin with the wand
waved it over the instruments. A shower
of ice crystals burst out. Immediately, all
the instruments
shrank down
until they
were tiny.
The goblins
laughed
and cheered.
"STOP!"
Poppy cried,
heading toward them
with Kirsty and Rachel close behind.

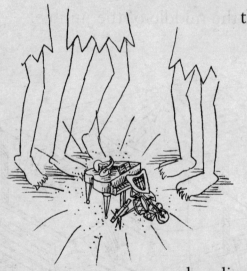

"No way!" the goblins jeered. They
each grabbed one of the tiny instruments

and dashed over to a window on the other side of the room.

"Ha ha ha!" laughed a familiar, icy voice. "The magical musical instruments are mine!"

A cold shiver ran down the girls' spines as they saw that Jack Frost was waiting for the goblins by the open window.

Jack Frost saw the girls and scowled.

"You're too late, you pesky humans!" he shouted. "You won't stop me this time!"

He pointed his wand out the window and shot a freezing blast of icy crystals in a downward stream. Within seconds, the crystals had formed an ice slide. The goblins whooped with glee and jumped onto the slide, still clutching the tiny instruments. Then they zipped down the slide. Poppy and the girls could only watch.

"Oh no!" Poppy gasped. "Jack Frost and his goblins are escaping with our magic musical instruments!"

"We can still stop them!" Rachel
shouted, sounding determined.

The three friends dashed across the
room toward the window, dodging
overturned chairs and music stands. But
as Jack Frost jumped onto the
slide himself, he
pointed his
ice wand
straight
at them.

"Quick!"
Poppy cried
out. "Hide!"
She grabbed the
girls' hands and
pulled them
behind a nearby
drum set.

Kirsty's heart was pounding as she
peeked around a drum, expecting to see
one of Jack Frost's ice bolts flying
toward them.

But to her surprise, she saw a cloud of
white paper spill from Jack Frost's wand.
It whirled around the room like confetti.

"How strange. It's just paper!" she
shouted to Poppy and Rachel. "Hurry,
Jack Frost is getting away!"

They all rushed out from behind the drum set. But there was so much paper, it was like flying through a snowy blizzard. Poppy and the girls could hardly see where they were going! As they struggled over to the window, they could just see Jack Frost sliding off into the distance. And as he zoomed away in a storm of snowflakes, they could hear him chanting a spell:

"Goblins stand out because they're green,
But I don't want them to be seen.
I cast this spell so they'll blend in,
Then girls and fairies will not win!"

"What does that mean?" Kirsty asked, frowning. Meanwhile, Rachel began to climb onto the ice slide, but Poppy grabbed her arm.

"It's not safe, Rachel," the fairy said urgently. "Look, the ice is melting."

Rachel could see that Poppy was right.

"Then what are we going to do?" she asked anxiously. "We can't let Jack Frost and his goblins get away with the instruments!"

"I need to tell the other Music Fairies right away," Poppy sighed. "Maybe we can come up with a plan. . . ."

Kirsty stared through the snowflakes spinning around outside the window. She could see the melting ice slide stretching far into the distance. At the end of the slide was something that looked very familiar. Kirsty frowned in concentration. Then she suddenly realized that the ice slide led to the bandstand in Wetherbury Park, not far from her house!

She was about to tell the others when Rachel let out a huge gasp. She'd picked up a handful of Jack Frost's paper confetti and was studying it more closely. "This isn't confetti!" she exclaimed. "The sheets of paper are tiny posters!" Kirsty and Poppy both picked up

pieces of confetti. Each poster had a picture of Jack Frost, with some writing underneath. Rachel read the words aloud.

"'Jack Frost invites you to see Frosty and his Gobolicious Band — appearing in the human world as stars of the National Talent Competition!'"

"We heard about that on the radio, Rachel!" Kirsty cried. "Jack Frost and his goblins are entering the competition? If he wins, Jack Frost will be a star!"

"Oh, he'd like that, wouldn't he?" Rachel commented with a grin. "Jack Frost would love to have all the power and glory of being a pop star!"

Poppy was looking very worried. "And unfortunately, with the help of our magic musical instruments, Frosty and his Gobolicious Band are going to perform fantastically!" she said sadly. "With fairy magic on his side, there's no way Jack Frost could lose. We have to get our instruments back before the competition begins!"

Out of Tune

Rachel and Kirsty looked worried.

"If Jack Frost wins, there will be a lot
of publicity," Kirsty pointed out. "It
won't take long for people to realize he's
not human, and then everyone will find
out that fairies really do exist!"

"Yes, Fairyland will be discovered,
and, with the magic musical instruments

stuck in the human world, music will be ruined for everyone, forever!" Poppy replied, her wings drooping sadly.

Suddenly, six other fairies rushed in through the open door.

"We came as soon as we got your message, Poppy!" one of them cried. "What happened?"

"Jack Frost escaped with our magic instruments," Poppy explained miserably, "even though Rachel, Kirsty, and I did our best to stop him. He plans to enter the National Talent Competition in the human world!"

The other fairies gasped in horror.

"Girls, meet the Music Fairies," Poppy

went on, turning to Rachel and Kirsty. "Ellie the Guitar Fairy, Fiona the Flute Fairy, Danni the Drum Fairy, Maya the Harp Fairy, Victoria the Violin Fairy, and Sadie the Saxophone Fairy."

"Thank you for coming," said Danni. "Will you help us get the instruments back?"

"Oh, please!" Fiona chimed in. "We can't imagine life in Fairyland or the human world without music."

"Of course we'll help," Kirsty said.

"We couldn't imagine life without music, either!" Rachel agreed.

"But where should we start looking?" asked Sadie.

Suddenly Kirsty remembered what she'd seen at the end of the ice slide. "I know exactly where Jack Frost has gone," she cried. "I saw that his ice slide led to the bandstand in Wetherbury Park!"

"Nice work, Kirsty!" Poppy declared. "Ellie, will you tell the king and queen about Jack Frost's latest mischief? I'll go with Rachel and Kirsty — they might need fairy magic to help them."

Ellie nodded. "And we'll clean up the school while you three find Jack Frost and his goblins." She pointed her wand at an overturned music stand. A shower of sparkles lifted it so it was right-side up again. The other Music Fairies joined in,

their magic making the sheet music, chairs, and instruments dance their way back to their proper places.

 Meanwhile, Poppy waved her wand over herself and the girls, and her magic immediately whisked them off to Wetherbury in a mist of rainbow sparkles.

A moment later, the girls found themselves back to their normal size. They were standing in the park next to the bandstand.

"Any sign of Jack Frost and his goblins?" Poppy murmured, hovering out of sight behind Kirsty's hair.

The girls looked around. Everything seemed pretty normal at first glance.

There was a man walking his dog, a couple of mothers with strollers chatting on a nearby bench, and a group of children playing on the swings.

But then Rachel noticed something weird. A young boy wearing strange clothes was standing near the bandstand. His bright yellow pants were too long, and his shirtsleeves were too short. He also wore a big, floppy, purple hat, which covered his face.

Rachel nudged Kirsty.

"Do you think that boy could be a goblin?" she whispered. "He's got a goblin's funny fashion sense!"

"Let's go and see," Kirsty replied.

Poppy and the girls went to get a better look. But as they got closer to the boy, Rachel shook her head.

"He can't be a goblin," she said. "Look at his arms — they're not green."

Poppy frowned. "I know my beautiful piano is nearby, girls," she said. "I can feel its music calling to me. But where is it?"

"Maybe the goblins already left the park," Kirsty suggested. "We could look along High Street. There are plenty of places to hide there."

Poppy nodded and flew into Kirsty's pocket, out of sight. The girls hurried toward the park gates. As they did, they passed the mothers sitting on the bench. One of them was singing a lullaby to her baby, who was crying.

"Hush, little baby, go to sleep," she warbled in a voice that was horribly off-key.

Kirsty and Rachel exchanged worried looks as the baby began to cry even louder.

37

Then, just outside the park gates, they saw a street performer playing the harmonica. But the tune sounded terrible. The man couldn't hit any of the right notes! The result was a horrible screeching, earsplitting noise.

"That's awful!" Rachel whispered to Kirsty, making a face as they passed by.

"I've seen that man playing here before, and he's usually really good," Kirsty replied. "This is all because the magic musical instruments are missing. Music everywhere is being ruined!"

"You're right!" Poppy exclaimed. "No one can sing or play instruments well anymore. We have to find Jack Frost and his goblins and return the instruments to Fairyland!"

High Street was near the park, and Rachel and Kirsty began going into stores and cafés, looking for goblins. As they searched, they heard how music was being ruined everywhere.

"Listen to that background music," Kirsty whispered to Rachel as they looked around the local bookstore. "It's terrible!"

Rachel nodded. "It sounds like someone screaming, not singing!" she replied.

"My MP3 player's not working," a teenage boy complained to his mom, pulling the headphones out of his ears.

"Even the car horns are honking off-key," Kirsty remarked as they went outside again.

"And the birds are singing out of tune!" Rachel pointed out.

The girls hurried down High Street, trying not to listen to the awful noises all around them. But suddenly they heard something else — a sweet, pure melody wafting toward them on the breeze.

Poppy gasped. "That's my piano!"

Goblin Surprise!

Rachel and Kirsty headed straight
toward the clear, beautiful sound of
Poppy's piano.

"It's coming from the music store!"
Kirsty announced breathlessly.

She and Rachel peeked through the
display window, expecting to spot a

goblin. But to their surprise, they saw the strangely-dressed boy from the park.

He was sitting on a stool in front of Poppy's piano, playing a very difficult piece of classical music.

"Look, my piano's full-size again!" Poppy whispered, peeking out of Kirsty's pocket. "Remember the wand the goblins had at the school? Jack Frost must have given them the power to change the size of our musical instruments. We can do that with our fairy magic, but usually the goblins can't."

The boy's fingers were flashing across the keys in a blur. He finished the piece with a flourish, swept off his floppy hat, and stood up to take a bow.

Kirsty and Rachel stared at him in disbelief.

"He *is* a goblin!" Kirsty exclaimed, peering at the boy's pointy ears and nose.

"But he's not green!" Rachel said, looking confused. "Oh!" Suddenly her eyes opened wide. "Remember Jack Frost's spell?

"Goblins stand out because they're green,
But I don't want them to be seen.

*I cast this spell so they'll blend in,
Then girls and fairies will not win!"*

Rachel grinned. "The goblins aren't green anymore. Jack Frost took the green out of their skin!" she declared.

"But they still look like goblins," Kirsty added. "They still have pointy noses and big feet and huge ears, so the spell didn't work completely!"

"And he has my piano!" Poppy said, staring longingly through the window. "How are we going to get it back?" They all looked at the

goblin, who was flexing his fingers, ready
to play another tune.

"I have an idea," Rachel said slowly.
"Maybe we should use the goblin's
disguise against him."

"How?" asked Kirsty.

"I can pretend
to be a goblin,
too!" Rachel
replied. "I'll tell
him Jack Frost
wants to see
him, so he can
promote him to lead
singer of the Gobolicious Band!"
She stared through the store window.
"Kirsty, you hide behind those big
speakers and I'll get the goblin to come
toward you."

"Then I'll think of a way to keep him busy while Poppy uses magic to send her piano back to Fairyland," Kirsty finished. "Great idea!"

"And guess what?" Poppy said, her eyes twinkling. "I can make your nose and ears a bit bigger, Rachel, so that you'll look more like a goblin!" Poppy immediately flew out of Kirsty's pocket and showered Rachel with fairy dust. Kirsty watched closely. She could hardly believe her eyes when Rachel's nose

began to grow to a long point. At the
same time, Rachel's ears grew bigger
and bigger until at last she looked
remarkably like a non-green goblin with
wavy golden hair!

Piano Plan

"How do I look?" Rachel asked, studying her reflection in the display window.

"Just like a goblin!" Kirsty replied. She grinned at Rachel and hurried into the music store. Rachel and Poppy waited for a moment until Kirsty had hidden herself safely behind the tall speakers.

Then Poppy flew behind Rachel's hair, and they went into the store.

First, Rachel checked that the shopkeepers were busy with customers before she headed over to the goblin. She knew she had to act quickly. Poppy's magic would wear off soon, and her nose and ears would shrink back to their normal size.

But as Rachel got closer to the goblin, he saw her coming. Frowning, he whipped a wand out of his pocket.

It's the wand the goblins used at the school!
Rachel thought, alarmed. *I'd better stop
him before he shrinks Poppy's piano again and
runs off with it!* The goblin lifted the wand.

"Wait!" Rachel called. "I'm a goblin,
too!" she added in a low voice.

The goblin stared suspiciously at her.

"How do I know you're a goblin?"
he asked.

"Look at our reflections," Rachel told
him, bending over the shiny piano top.
She was really glad that Poppy had
altered her features with fairy magic!

"We both look human,
don't we?"

The goblin nodded, still suspicious.

"Well, you look human but you're actually a goblin," Rachel went on. "And I look human, too, so I must be a goblin like you, right?"

The goblin looked very confused. Rachel desperately hoped that he wouldn't think too carefully about what she'd just said. She was relying on the fact that goblins weren't very smart! "Right," the goblin agreed at last, and Rachel tried not to sigh

with relief. "We've got the same ears and the same nose. But . . ." He frowned at Rachel's jeans and T-shirt.

"My human clothes are much nicer than yours!"

"Oh, they're very nice and bright," Rachel assured him, trying not to giggle.

"Yes, I like the clothes, but my skin is awfully plain," the goblin grumbled. "I miss being green. Green is such a beautiful color!"

Rachel tried to hide her smile.

"I miss being green, too," she replied. "But you know how the Gobolicious Band is entering the National Talent Competition? Well, Jack Frost wants to see you right away. I think he's planning to promote you to lead singer!"

"Me?" Looking
tremendously
excited,
the goblin
bounced up
and down
on the
piano stool.
"He's right —
I'd be a great
lead singer! My
good looks are wasted behind this piano!"

This time Rachel had to bite her lip to
stop herself from laughing.

"Jack Frost is waiting for you over
there," she said, pointing at the speakers
where Kirsty was hiding.

"Hooray!" the goblin whooped. He
jumped up and rushed across the store.

Anxiously, Rachel glanced at Poppy, who was already peeking out from behind her hair. Would Kirsty be able to stall the goblin long enough for them to send the piano back to Fairyland?

Get That Goblin!

Behind the speakers, Kirsty was waiting. Her heart thumped. She still hadn't decided how to stop the goblin from rushing back to the piano when he realized it was all a trick.

But suddenly, she spotted a stand holding a microphone that had a long cord attached to it.

Carefully, Kirsty removed the microphone from the stand and took the cord in both hands. Peeking around the speakers, she saw the goblin dashing toward her.

Here goes! Kirsty thought.

As the goblin rushed around the side of the speakers, Kirsty was ready with the

microphone cord. Before the goblin realized what was happening, she'd wrapped the cord tightly around him, once, twice, then a third time. "Hey!" the goblin yelled, looking very confused. "Where's Jack Frost?"

"That's what we'd like to know!"
Kirsty replied, whizzing around and
around the goblin several more times
until he was completely wrapped up in
the microphone cord, like a package tied
with string.

By this time, the goblin realized he was
trapped. He shrieked with rage and tried
to get free, but Kirsty held on tightly to
both ends of the cord.

Suddenly, a sweet melody filled the air.
Kirsty stepped out from behind the
speakers and saw Poppy flying across the
keyboard of her piano. Dazzling fairy
dust fell from her wand onto the keys.
The magic sparkles made
beautiful music!

"Give me my piano!" the goblin squealed furiously. He lunged forward so forcefully that he pulled the cord from Kirsty's hands. But it was too late. With a final tinkling melody, the piano vanished in a swirl of fairy magic. Poppy smiled happily at Rachel and Kirsty.

"Thank you, girls!" she said gratefully.

Looking sulky, the goblin was untangling himself from the microphone cord.

"Does this mean I don't get to be lead singer?" he demanded.

"I'm afraid not," Poppy replied.

The goblin snorted in disgust. "I could have been a megastar if it weren't for you mean girls!" he muttered as he stomped off.

Poppy laughed. "I hope you'll be able to help the other Music Fairies find their musical instruments, girls," she went on. "A world without music would be no fun at all, would it?" She waved at

Rachel and Kirsty. "Good-bye — and good luck!"

"Good-bye, Poppy," the girls chorused as their fairy friend disappeared in a puff of glitter and a swirl of tinkling piano music.

"Poppy's right," Rachel said, gazing around at all the instruments in the store. "The world wouldn't be the same without music."

"Then we have to stop Jack Frost from winning the competition!" Kirsty replied in a determined voice. She grinned at Rachel. "Besides, I don't think the human world is ready for Frosty and his Gobolicious Band!"

THE MUSIC FAIRIES

Poppy the Piano Fairy's magic
instrument is safe and sound in
Fariyland! Can Rachel and Kirsty help

Ellie
the Guitar Fairy?

Join their next adventure in this special
sneak peek. . . .

Guitar Star

Rachel Walker smiled across the breakfast table at her best friend, Kirsty Tate. "Yesterday was a really great start to school break, wasn't it?" she said. "I love spending our vacations together. We always have the best adventures!"

Kirsty nodded. "Did you just hear something?" she asked.

The two girls sat in silence for a moment, listening.

"It sounds like bells," Rachel said in surprise. "Or a tambourine!" Her eyes lit up as she turned to Kirsty.

"I don't remember there being a magic tambourine," Kirsty replied in a low voice, looking puzzled. Then the kitchen door opened, and her face broke into a grin. "Dad — it's you!"

Mr. Tate came into the room, shaking a tambourine enthusiastically. "Morning, girls!" he said cheerfully.

"Do you have band practice now?" Kirsty asked.

Mr. Tate grinned. "I sure do," he said. "Your ears are in for a treat!"

Kirsty laughed as he left the room. "I wouldn't call it a treat," she told Rachel.

"They're not very good. And now that
the fairies' instruments are missing, Dad's
band is going to sound even worse than
usual!"

"Your dad's band can't be that bad,"
Rachel said, getting to her feet. "Let's go
and listen."

The two girls left the kitchen and went
outside to the barn that stood a short
distance from the Tates' house. They
peeked around the door.

"What a racket!" Kirsty whispered to
Rachel. "We've got to find those other
missing instruments. This is one band that
really needs help!"

There's Magic in Every Series!

The Rainbow Fairies

The Weather Fairies

The Jewel Fairies

The Pet Fairies

The Fun Day Fairies

The Petal Fairies

The Dance Fairies

The Music Fairies

The Sports Fairies

The Party Fairies

Read them all!

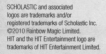

RAINBOW magic™

THE RAINBOW FAIRIES

Find the magic in every book!

RAINBOW magic™

SPECIAL EDITION

Three Books in One— More Rainbow Magic Fun!

■SCHOLASTIC
www.scholastic.com
www.rainbowmagiconline.com

HiT entertain

RMSPEC